DISNEY'S
THE
WILD

The Junior Novelization

Library of Congress Control Number: 2004103555

ISBN: 0-7364-2298-6

ISBN-13: 978-0-7364-2298-7

The text of this book is set in 13-point Times.

www.randomhouse.com/kids/disney

Printed in the United States of America

10 9 8 7 6 5 4 3 2 1

DISNEY's THE WILD

The Junior Novelization

Adapted by Irene Trimble

Random House 🏠 New York

Chapter 1

In the haze of a summer afternoon, two lions stretched across a sunbaked rock. A warm wind blew through the larger lion's mane as he stood and looked into the distance. His name was Samson, and he was known for being the most ferocious lion for many miles around.

He was also known for his exciting stories of adventure. "It all started," Samson said with a swagger, "in a little place I like to call the Wild."

Young Ryan listened as his father told him stories of the great hunts on the plains of Africa. Ryan could almost feel the ground tremble with the thunder of hooves from the vast herds of fleeing wildebeests.

"We're talking *fast,*" Samson said, describing a chase. "All the other lions had given up the hunt hours ago, except your old man," he said to Ryan with a wink. "Fortunately, I knew a shortcut."

Ryan's father described how he single-handedly chased a wild herd into a gorge.

"I thought I had 'em—until the dust cleared. Classic wildebeest trap," said the old-timer.

"That's when I gave them the roar!" Samson bellowed a loud roar. Ryan's ears flattened against his head as his father unleashed the earth-shattering sound. He believed that those beasts must have fallen like dominos when they heard that terrible roar.

"That's it?" Ryan asked, anticipating more.

"I only thought it was over," Samson said, smiling. "But they had a secret weapon," he continued.

Samson and Ryan jumped from the rock and crouched in the tall grass.

"He was the biggest wildebeest I had ever seen!" Samson declared as they peered through the grass.

Ryan paid close attention, even though he had heard this story many times before.

"He was fourteen feet tall!" Samson exclaimed.

Ryan's ears tilted up. "Fourteen?" He remembered a different version.

"I meant fourteen hundred and one feet tall," Samson said quickly. "And he had two . . . no, four of the biggest horns I'd ever seen!" Ryan's eyes grew wide as Samson explained that the animal's very breath could set the trees of the savannah on fire.

"To pull this off, I knew I was gonna have to dig

deep," Samson told his son. "Deeper than I ever had before. So I swallowed my fear, sucked in the biggest breath I could . . ."

Ryan knew that this was where his dad's big roar came in. He took in a big breath himself. "Dad, I'm ready. I can do it!" he shouted, ready to roar like a huge lion.

"Well, let him have it!" said Samson. "Roar, son!"

The young lion pushed out of the weeds. He threw his head back and opened his mouth, and out came a scratchy squeak.

The crowd outside the lion enclosure pointed at Ryan and laughed. Samson suddenly let out a ferocious roar to quiet them.

"Story of my life," Ryan said as the zoo visitors clapped for Samson's booming voice. "Your roar stops a herd of wildebeests. Mine makes the babies laugh."

"Hey, c'mon," Samson said, "that was much better. I'm serious; it dropped half an octave. And it sure scared me. I mean, look." Samson held out his giant paw and tried to blow on the fur without Ryan seeing. "Made my hair stand up on end!"

Ryan shrugged. "Yeah, right, Dad," he said, and walked toward his favorite tree.

Samson went after him and tried to get him to roar

again. "Come on. Let's take it from the top. You were so close." He pulled Ryan's cheeks to make his jaw wide. "Maybe it's something technical. Maybe you're not opening your mouth wide enough. You've got to roar to the wildebeests in the back row."

The young lion pulled away from his father. "If you really wanted me to roar like you, you'd take me to the Wild."

Samson was stunned. "Whoa, hold on a sec. We've got everything we could ever want right here! A great lifestyle, three squares a day . . ."

"And it's boring," Ryan said flatly. "I'm never going to learn how to roar here, Dad. But don't worry, I finally figured out how we can get to the Wild."

"You did?"

Ryan nodded enthusiastically. "The pigeons say those green boxes go there!"

"Ryan, listen. I know you're frustrated, but a lion finds his roar . . ."

Ryan pointed to his heart. "Here?" he asked impatiently. The big lion nodded. "Ooohh! I'm so tired of hearing that, Dad!"

Samson and Ryan suddenly heard a woman scream, "Aaaagh! Get that rat off my baby!"

Outside the lion enclosure, Benny the squirrel was

desperately trying to snatch a candy bracelet from the hands of a baby in a stroller. Benny stopped pulling for a second. "A rat?" he asked, insulted.

The woman raised her purse and swung. The blow knocked Benny onto the pavement, where he landed with a thud. "Rats don't got bling like this, lady!" said the angry squirrel, shaking the candy bracelet in his fist.

He put up his paws in a fighting stance when— *whap!*—the purse came down again and launched him into the air.

Benny tumbled over the lion enclosure and right into Samson's nose.

"Benny," said Samson, sounding as if he had a head cold, "stealing candy from a baby?" He sneezed out his small friend, right into Ryan's open paw.

"Hey, kid," Benny said, turning to Ryan. "Heard the roar. Down another octave. So are you ready to cheer me and your old man as we capture our fifth straight turtle-curling title?" he asked. That night's game was a huge sporting event. All the animals wanted to see if Samson's team would remain undefeated.

"I can't even roar. How would you know I'm there?" Ryan asked. He turned and headed for his tree.

Samson watched his son disappear in the branches. "So you really think it dropped an octave?" he asked Benny, hoping his son's roar really had gotten a little better.

"Absolutely," Benny reassured his friend. "What the heck is an octave?"

Chapter 2

At feeding time, Ryan still hadn't come down from his tree.

"I just don't know what his problem is, Benny," Samson said, ripping at a piece of meat from the feeding drawer. "He's eleven, but he's still roaring at a nine-year-old level."

Benny took a bite of his own dinner, a meaty little acorn. "Maybe you're setting the bar too high for him with all your stories about Samson the Wild."

"Hey. He's always loved those stories. They inspire him."

"Okay, okay," Benny agreed. "I'm not gonna argue with someone who could use my tail as dental floss." He suddenly made a face. "Um, Sammy," he said, raising his tiny lip and pointing at his front tooth, "you got something here."

Samson was about to use his giant claw as a toothpick when a voice announcing the zoo's closing came over the loudspeaker.

"Attention, friends," it blared, "before you leave, stop by the gift shop and get the most popular plush in America, Nigel, the *I Like You* koala. And have a really nice day!"

As the zoo visitors happily clutched their Nigel plush toys and headed for the exits, Samson and Benny breathed a sigh of relief. Benny craned his neck up and looked around. "Finally," he said, "the zoo will officially be ours in T-minus three, two . . ." He could see the lights of the city begin to twinkle as the zookeeper pulled the main gate shut for the night. "And . . . showtime!" Benny said as an elephant raised his trunk and trumpeted with all his might.

With all the humans finally gone for the night, every animal in the zoo quietly hurried toward the ice for the curling competition.

A chubby little koala named Nigel—the one the toy was named for—tried to leap over a fence from his tree. Unfortunately, he got caught on the fence, fell to the ground, and was stomped by an elephant. But he kept on going.

In the zoo's fountain, a giant anaconda named Larry squeezed from a huge marble spout shaped like an elephant's trunk.

At the same time, a group of pink flamingos used

the long neck of a giraffe as a ramp to make their escape. The giraffe's name was Bridget, and she patiently waited as the flamingos scurried up her neck and over the fence.

Despite their huge difference in size, Benny the squirrel had a crush on Bridget. He was determined to ask her out.

He rushed up to her with the candy bracelet and said, "This is for you, honey. It goes around your left hoof."

"Did you get that out of the trash? You trash picker!" she said, rebuffing the love-struck squirrel.

"I'm not a trash picker. I'm a recycler," he joked. "That's a lot more romantic, isn't it?"

"Don't mention romance to me, Benny. I've never had a boyfriend," shot back the giraffe.

"Great! That settles it. I accept the job of boyfriend number one!" said the brazen squirrel.

But Bridget wasn't interested in the small furry animal.

"Benny, only the female orb-weaver spider will date a male one-twentieth her size," she said, dashing his hopes.

The animals came from all corners of the zoo. No one wanted to miss that night's all-zoo curling championship!

Ryan's friends, a young kangaroo named Duke and a hippo named Eze, had made their escape as well. They met up on the main path, and both said, "Let's get Ryan, dude."

Duke and Eze cracked up. "Dude, we said it at the same time!" They high-fived, shouting, "Duuude!" and headed off to find Ryan.

Chapter 3

At the gate to the lion enclosure, Samson greeted his passing fans.

An adoring giraffe called out, "You're the king, Samson!"

"Curl those turtles old school, cat," said a beaming elephant.

Samson waved and exchanged high fives with his fans. "Samson's the name, see you at the game," he shouted, enjoying the animals' admiration.

"Listen, I'm heading down to the game," he called up to Ryan. "I'm going to see you there, then, right? We need you. You're our biggest fan."

But Ryan didn't answer. He knew he'd never be half the lion his dad was. How could he be, just hanging around a zoo all his life?

"Ryan, listen, about this afternoon . . . ," Samson said.

"Dad! Fine. I'll go to your game, all right?"

Samson didn't know what to do. "Okay," he called up. "Guess I'll see you there, then." The big lion joined the other animals heading down the park path.

Ryan was feeling more depressed than ever when he heard, "Psst! Dude! Guess who's heeere?"

"Eze! Duke!" Ryan shouted excitedly.

Duke laughed. "Man, he always guesses!"

"We're gonna stalk the gazelles while everybody's at the game," Duke told Ryan. "You in?"

"I'm coming down," said Ryan as he watched the animals on the path make way for his dad.

Chapter 4

In the center of the zoo, an ice-skating rink had turned into an arena for the big game. Under the light of the moon, the all-zoo curling championship was in full swing. The stands were packed with cheering fans. "Fish heads! Get your ice-cold fish heads!" a flamingo called as he tossed one to a hungry rhinoceros.

A small bow-tied penguin was clutching his microphone and calling the game over the roar of the crowd. "Folks, we're heading into the final period, and the penguins are up. Here comes Victor." The captain of the penguin team was a fierce competitor.

Samson was in an ice dugout, trying to rally his team. They were feeling pretty low. Bridget the giraffe, Larry the snake, Nigel the koala, and, of course, Benny the squirrel all cringed when they heard the announcer pump the crowd.

"The penguins are going to be tough to beat," said the announcer.

"Tough to beat?" yelled Samson. "That's just the

way we like it. Right, guys?" They weren't so sure.

"If we lose, I'm gonna rip my head off!" Nigel said, pacing around the dugout. "And yours!" he shouted at a passing penguin.

"We cannot lose to flightless birds!" Bridget sneered.

It was up to Samson to pull the team together. "Whoa," he called out. "No one's losing anything 'round here as long as we stay focused."

Then, glancing around distractedly, he asked, "Has anyone seen Ryan?"

"Oh, I know," the snake said. "Maybe he's sulking 'cause he lives in his father's shadow and he roars like a schoolgirl!"

"Thanks, Lar," Samson answered dully.

"Nigel, will you sign my dolly?" an adoring monkey fan in the crowd called out. Nigel turned. She was holding up an *I Like You* Nigel doll.

Soon a line of monkeys formed behind her, all of them waving their little stuffed koalas. "Oh, not again," Nigel moaned. He'd grown tired of the fame.

The monkeys kept pulling the string on the doll's back. Nigel heard his own voice singing, "I'm so cuddly. I like you," over and over.

"You're so cuddly. We like you!" the monkeys

chanted together, pointing at Nigel.

Nigel had had it. "That's it! I am not cuddly. I'm a vicious jungle animal, from the streets of London," he sneered at the crowd. "Fear me!"

He struck a fierce karate position. But that didn't calm the monkeys down. They reached into the dugout and grabbed him.

"Help me!" Nigel screamed. The koala clung to Bridget's horn with all his might.

"Girls—girls, put him down!" Samson yelled.

The monkeys laughed as they searched Nigel's fur with their paws. "Find his string, find his string. . . . ," they screamed.

"Nigel doesn't have a string," Bridget said, leaning in to see what the monkeys were looking for.

Nigel grabbed both of Bridget's horns as the monkeys pinched him all over. "Aaagh! Leave my bum alone!" poor Nigel cried.

"Hey! Get your paws off my girlfriend!" Benny shouted to the monkeys, who were now swinging from Bridget's neck.

Bridget swung her neck around and lost her balance. "Benny," she shouted as she fell, "I can handle myself—whaaaa!"

Benny scurried to avoid the avalanche of monkeys

followed by a terrified koala and a huge giraffe, but he didn't move fast enough.

The crowd gasped as Bridget landed on Benny with a splat. "What is up with Samson's team tonight?" the announcer shouted as Bridget scrambled to her feet.

She looked down at the poor flattened squirrel. "Benny . . . Benny . . . ," she said, but Benny's eyes didn't open. "Omigosh! Who knows mouth-to-mouth?"

Benny popped up. "I do!" he said, and planted a big kiss on her mouth.

Bridget was stunned. She had no interest in dating Benny. "Elch. What was that?" she asked, shaking her big head.

"Just your daily dose of vitamin Benny, baby," the happy squirrel said with a gleam in his eye.

Meanwhile, a frustrated Nigel, standing on Bridget's back, was busy pummeling a stuffed koala.

The toy kept repeating, "I'm so cuddly. I like you," until Nigel couldn't take it anymore. "Stop saying that!" Nigel shouted, giving the toy one more mighty wallop.

Larry took that moment to spring like a cannonball and give the group a hug—a hug that sent the team tumbling to the ground, on top of Samson, who shook his head.

"Next year I should just coach," said the flattened lion.

Things did not look promising for Samson's ragtag team.

Chapter 5

At the same time, in another part of the zoo, Ryan was crouching in the tall grass with Duke and Eze.

"Check it. The Thomson gazelle," Eze whispered as they eyed the nervous herd.

Duke nodded. "Zero to fifty in four-point-five seconds. The ultimate fleeing machine."

Duke took a step toward the herd. "Maybe we should just go to the game," Ryan said cautiously.

Eze and Duke turned to Ryan. "I thought you wanted to be wild, dude!" said Eze.

"I bet your dad chased gazelles," Duke challenged.

"Yeah, if he were our age, he would be so rockin' out with us," Eze continued.

"Yeah! He'd already be in there," Duke said excitedly, "running 'em down like they were . . ."

"Gazelles," Eze said.

"Yeah, gazelles or something," Duke agreed.

"We'd better not," Ryan said as Duke and Eze edged out of the reeds toward the herd.

"Oh, yeah?" Duke said. "You gonna stop us?" The hippo and the kangaroo were ready to pounce. "On three, dude," Duke whispered. "One, two . . ."

"Noooo!" Ryan *rooooarr*ed and leaped over his friends to keep them from charging. But it was too late. The gazelles were frightened of the roar of a lion, even if it was a scratchy little roar.

"Uh-oh," said Duke as the herd began to stampede. "Now you did it, Ryan."

Meanwhile, back at the game, Samson's team took to the ice. "Samson's gotta throw a bull's-eye here, folks!" the announcer told the crowd. Every fan was glued to the red target on the ice. Could Samson hit it?

"There's no tomorrow," the announcer said. "It's do or die. Ya know what I mean."

The members of Samson's team were feeling pretty low as they huddled on the ice. But Samson wasn't about to give up. "Guys, guys! I know we're down, but we're gonna pull this out." He suddenly got a gleam in his eye and declared, "'Cause we're gonna use"—then he whispered—"the secret play."

"The secret play!" Larry shouted excitedly. "HEY, EVERYONE, GUESS WHAT? WE'RE GONNA USE THE SECRET PLAY!"

"Larry," Bridget said, hoping everyone in New York hadn't heard the news, "the first part of the secret play? Keeping it secret."

"Just follow my lead," Samson told them. "I need a double effort from everybody!"

"Absolutely," Nigel promised with a salute. "Triple effort if you want, sir."

"Good," Samson said. "Ready and . . ."

"Break!" they all shouted in unison as they high-fived each other.

Samson appeared on the ice with a turtle in his hand. All he had to do was whack the turtle, named Donald, into the red goal at the end of the arena.

The team got into position for the secret play. Larry the snake wound his tail end around Benny and his neck end around Bridget, turning himself into the perfect slingshot. Samson got into position, too. "Feelin' mean, Donald?" he asked, looking down at the turtle.

"Bring it oooooon!" Donald told him as Samson stretched Larry back and loaded up the turtle. Benny dug his front teeth into the ice as Samson pulled. Suddenly, Victor, from Team Penguin, yelled, "Hey, Samson, it's a shame your little brat isn't here to see you lose."

Samson froze.

"I caaaan't hooooold . . . ," Benny grunted, trying to keep his teeth in the ice.

As Benny's grip failed, Larry's tail whipped

toward Samson. The huge lion jumped out of the way as Larry's tail swung and wrapped around Bridget's neck.

Samson grabbed the turtle and hurled him over the heads of the swarming penguins. "And here comes Samson!" the announcer called. "Is he a beauty or what?"

"Larry, Bridget, sweep!" Samson roared as Donald the turtle slid toward the bull's-eye.

Bridget's long steps kept her ahead of the sliding turtle as Larry, still wrapped around her neck, swept the path clear.

"Sweep faster, Larry!" Bridget called over her shoulder. "Sweep! Sweep! Sweep!"

A stocky thug of a penguin took to the ice. "Team Penguin is sending their ace, Victor, to slow the turtle down," the announcer told the crowd, "while Samson's crew is doin' their best to keep it moving!"

Larry and Bridget were locked broom to broom with Victor. "Watch it!" Larry shouted to the penguin.

"Watch it yourself!" Victor called back.

Nigel was observing the action from behind the goal. "Move left a bit!" he shouted to Larry.

But Larry misunderstood the little koala. "Okay," Larry yelled, "move left and HIT!"

"Larry, NO!" Bridget screamed.

"Oh," Larry said, nodding, "TALLYHO!" and he whacked the turtle with all his might.

The crowd watched as the turtle ricocheted all over the ice, bounced off Nigel's forehead, then slid toward the bull's-eye.

The crowd held their breath. "Folks, we are inches away from the greatest upset in turtle-curling history!" the announcer called.

"Go on," Samson yelled as the turtle inched his way to the bull's-eye.

"Yes!" Samson cheered.

"Unbelievable!" the announcer shouted to the roaring crowd. "Samson and his team have clinched the title again! But wait. I called it too soon."

Bridget, Larry, Nigel, and Benny were about to jump for joy when the turtle suddenly began to wobble. It shook back and forth until it wobbled completely out of the bull's-eye.

"What the heck . . . ?" Samson said to himself, feeling the ice tremble.

"No! The penguins have done it! They're zoo champs for the first time ever!" the announcer said as Donald began to bounce away from the tee and down the ice.

Then Samson realized what could make the ground shake like that. "Stampede," he whispered.

Over the noise of the crowd, Samson roared, "STAMPEDE!"

Chapter 7

The thunder of hooves became louder and louder. The crowd turned to see Ryan desperately waving his paws at the charging herd.

"Pleeease! Stop!" Ryan shouted. But the gazelles ran until they hit the ice and slid in every direction.

Duke shook his head. "Busted."

"Catastrophic," Eze said, cringing as Ryan slid across the ice and skidded to a stop at Samson's feet. Samson let out a huge roar.

Ryan nervously looked up at his father and tried to smile. "Told you I'd come to the game."

"You think this is funny?" said Samson sternly. "You just endangered everyone in the zoo. . . ."

"I'm sorry. . . ."

"For what?" Samson asked, still angry. "Chasing the gazelles? Or costing us the game?"

Ryan wanted to explain, but he didn't know how.

"What's the problem?" Samson asked him. "All you do is sit up in your tree and sulk. I mean, what is it? Is all this 'cause you can't roar?"

Samson could see he'd hurt Ryan's feelings. "Ryan, I didn't mean that. . . ."

"You know what I'm doing when I'm sulking up in my tree, Dad? I'm thinking how great it would be if Samson the Wild wasn't my father . . . 'cause it'd sure make being Ryan the Lame a whole lot easier."

Ryan ran off into the night as Samson called, "Ryan! Ryan, I'm sorry! Please don't leave."

Larry the snake moved alongside Samson. "Bye, Ryan!" he shouted, smiling. "Thanks for coming to the game!" The clueless snake looked into Samson's big face. "And you were worried that he wouldn't show up."

Later that evening, Samson paced around the zoo fountain as Benny paced on the fountain's spout.

"I don't know what to do anymore, Benny. I've tried everything," the worried lion said.

Benny stopped pacing and looked at Samson. "Everything," Benny said. "You've tried everything?"

"What are you saying?" Samson asked.

"I'm saying you have to tell him the truth."

Samson shook his huge head as he thought about this. "I don't think I can do that. I mean, what's he going to think of me?"

"I don't know," Benny answered. "But if you don't tell him, you're gonna lose him, Sammy."

Samson knew that his friend was right, but he didn't know how to tell his son his secret.

Chapter 8

As Samson slowly walked back to the lion enclosure, Ryan walked along the zoo fence alone. Ryan passed a poster of his dad, the mighty Samson. The headlines describing his dad said, "Fierce, proud, and wild."

Ryan tried to pose like his father. He held up his paw and growled. But he knew he didn't measure up. *I'll never be a ferocious lion,* he was thinking when something caught his eye on the other side of the fence.

"The green boxes!" Ryan said in awe. He knew what he had to do.

He climbed a tall tree alongside the fence. Signs saying NO TRESSPASSING—RESRICTED AREA were posted, but Ryan jumped the fence anyway. He crept toward a green box with an open door and ducked inside to rest.

Back at the lion environment, Samson decided that it was time to talk to his son. He felt bad for yelling at Ryan earlier, and he wanted to clear the air and speak honestly. When he got to the top of Ryan's tree, he was shocked to see that it was empty. But some men working in the restricted area below caught his eye.

Samson heard the door slam on a green box. A human voice yelled, "Okay, they're all loaded up. Let's get movin'!"

A truck marked ZOO TO AFRICA RESCUE roared its engine and began to move.

"Wait!" Ryan yelled. "I don't wanna go! Help me!"

Samson could hear his son calling for help as he ran toward the zoo fence. "DAAAD!" Ryan cried.

"Ryan!" Samson roared.

"Dad, help me!" Ryan yelled through the bars of the green box. He could see his world getting farther and farther away.

Samson roared with all his might as the truck pulled away and Ryan disappeared.

Samson's team rushed up behind him. Quickly, he turned to Benny. "We need to have that truck followed!" Samson exclaimed. "Get me . . . the pigeons."

Chapter 9

Benny knew there was only one place to look for the pigeons. Behind the gift shop, they were playing an intense game of dice.

"Aaaahhhh . . . I am wanting snake eyes!" Hamir the pigeon howled. "Come on, baby."

But only two dots came up on the ladybugs used as dice, and Hamir threw his wings over his head. "Oh, Shiva! I am the great loser of all time! What offerings must I make, I wonder—"

"Hamir, Hamir," Benny said, grabbing the pigeon. "Get a grip on yourself!"

"Benny!" the poor pigeon said sorrowfully. "I am needing till Friday before I am paying you back!"

"No, no," Benny said as Samson approached. "It's Ryan! He's in one of those green boxes and they took it away on a truck! We've gotta find him!"

Hamir gasped. "That is not good. Not good at all," he said to Samson.

Hamir's wife cooed. "I am telling him, you crazy

pigeon! The green boxes go to the big water where..." Hamir nodded quickly. "Where the stiff lady with the spikes on her head."

Samson and Benny looked at each other, confused. "Spikes," Hamir repeated, using his wing feathers to make a crown above his head.

Samson took Hamir by the neck and raised the pigeon up to his nose. "Just tell me where the green boxes go," Samson said slowly.

"Stiff lady, spikes . . . ," Hamir answered, terrified.

Hamir's wife began flapping frantically and pointed toward the gift shop.

"Yes! Like my wife says," Hamir said, nodding, "the truck takes them to her! To her!"

Samson and Benny both turned toward the gift shop window. Next to a mountain of *I Like You* Nigel dolls was a shelf of green Statue of Liberty souvenirs. Each one had a torch in her hand and a crown on her head. Samson and Benny were still confused.

"Though I hate telling bad news," Hamir continued as Samson set him down, "there is more bad news to tell. When the sun rises, the green boxes leave on a boat-boat and never return."

Samson and Benny were stunned. "I am sorry for

this," Hamir said, staring at his toes. "I really am." But when he looked up, Samson and Benny had already taken off.

"Hellooo?" Hamir called into the darkness.

Chapter 10

Samson paced anxiously along the zoo fence. All he could think about was how to get to that boat. Then he eyed the large green Dumpster in the loading area. He knew that a truck came and took the garbage from the zoo every morning.

Bridget leaned her head over the fence, looked at the Dumpster, and got the same idea. "So when do we leave, Sammy?" she asked.

Samson knew how dangerous this was going to be. "It's not *we*," he told Bridget. "It's *me*. Let's make this clear," he announced to everyone. "This is now a rescue mission and I'm the only one going."

"We'll come, too!" Larry insisted. "We're not afraid! Are we, guys?"

"Afraid?" Nigel asked, trying to laugh it off. "No," he said, wrapping his short arms around his furry body. "You know koalas. More like . . . scared of things."

"Look, Ryan's like a cub to all of us," Bridget said

to Samson. "Not that I'll ever have my own at this rate."

"You want to leave with me? Okay," Samson told them. "If you don't mind being hunted down, shot at, stuffed . . ."

"Okay!" Larry said excitedly.

"Nobody's leaving but me," Samson emphasized. "Got it?"

The little gang looked around at their cozy zoo home. "Absolutely," Nigel said with a little salute. "You're the boss; you've got the big hair."

Benny hopped over to Samson and pointed back at Nigel, Larry, and Bridget. "Way to weed out the weak links," he said. "Now that they're out of the picture, what's the plan?"

Samson didn't say a word. Instead, he leaped over the fence and into the Dumpster, with Benny close behind him.

Chapter 11

Samson and Benny felt the Dumpster being raised by the huge garbage truck. Along with the zoo's garbage, Samson and Benny were tossed into the back of the truck. They could hear the hum of the motor as the truck slowly pulled out of the zoo's driveway and headed toward the city.

The truck bumped along the road as they hid in the bags of garbage. Finally, Samson raised his head and looked out the top of the truck. The zoo gates were behind him now, and the huge lion felt uncertain.

"Don't worry about a thing, big guy," Benny said confidently. "I got this all taken care of. I know this city like the back of my paw."

As Benny enjoyed a fairly clean lollipop he'd found, he told Samson, "We ditch this truck at Fifth Avenue. Couple lefts, couple rights, bada-boom, past Broadway, and—BAM!" All of a sudden, Bridget popped out of the trash, hurling the talkative squirrel clear out of the truck.

"What are you doing here?" Samson asked Bridget, not even noticing that Benny was gone.

The wind was making her large lips flap as she spoke. "Bleer blowing bloo blellu blind Blyan."

"What?" Samson asked.

"She said, 'We're going to help you find Ryan,'" Larry yelled, slithering between the garbage bags.

"Oh, great," Samson sighed. Then he felt something move underneath him. He reached down and pulled Nigel out of the trash.

The little koala had a popcorn bucket stuck around his waist. "I've got popcorn in my bum," Nigel said, modeling the red-and-white-striped bucket. "Do I look trashy in this?"

Samson sighed again and pulled the bucket off Nigel. "I only have until sunrise before Ryan is taken away forever, and now I have to worry about you three?"

Samson knew that from that moment on they were all in it together. "All right," he said. "When do we get off this thing, Benny?"

"B-b-b-b-enny's here?" Bridget said.

"Yeah, he's right there," Samson said, looking around, but there was no sign of the little squirrel.

"Benny?" Samson called out. Then he noticed

Benny's lollipop stuck to the edge of the truck.

"Great," Samson said, nodding. "Now what am I gonna do?"

"Guybs? I thig we shoulb GRUCK," Bridget suggested.

"What is she saying?" Samson asked.

Larry leaned out the truck and saw what Bridget was talking about. "She said . . . DUCK!" he yelled as the truck zoomed into a tunnel.

They huddled down, bumping along in the darkness.

"Whoa, hey?" Bridget shrieked. "All right, who's getting fresh down there?"

"That wasn't my paw. It was this," Nigel said, whipping out a souvenir Statue of Liberty torch. He flicked it on.

The light from the little torch lit up Samson's, Bridget's, and Larry's surprised faces. They all knew that the torch had come from the zoo gift shop.

"I didn't steal it," Nigel told them, in case they weren't sure. "I borrowed it. It'll light the way to Ryan."

Samson was about to laugh when the truck barreled out of the tunnel. Samson, Larry, Bridget, and Nigel looked up in awe.

The truck was on the streets of New York, a world made of steel and flashing lights, with buildings so high even Bridget couldn't see the tops of them.

As they rolled through Times Square, Bridget saw a huge billboard featuring a handsome giraffe. She was trying to read the sign when a loud hiss came from the truck's engine. The truck stopped so quickly that Samson, Bridget, Nigel, and Larry tumbled back into the garbage.

Suddenly, the truck began to make a horrible grinding noise. "That doesn't sound good," Bridget said, looking from side to side.

"Whoa," Larry said in shock. "The walls are moving."

"Oh, right, right," Bridget answered, not believing him, "the walls . . ." Then she saw the flat gray walls inch closer as the garbage began to press against her body. "The walls are moving!"

Samson had to think fast. He grabbed Larry. "Hold your breath!" he told him. Samson tried to position the stiffened snake like a pole between the moving walls. It held them back for only a second.

"Everybody out!" Samson shouted as the walls began to close in even faster.

"All right," Nigel answered, bumping around in the trash until Samson picked him up and tossed him over the edge of the truck.

"This is definitely not good!" Bridget said, pan-icked, as Samson and Larry struggled to get her out. But Bridget was just too large, and the space was get-ting smaller and smaller.

Suddenly, Samson reached for Larry and threw him into the air. Larry was completely surprised. *Thwunk*— he landed on the windshield of the garbage truck.

The driver was eye to eye with an enormous ana-conda. As he abandoned the truck, screaming, "AAAAHHHHHH! Garbage snake!" the hiss of the compactor finally came to a stop.

Bridget sighed and dropped her head. She'd almost been crushed!

Samson opened a trapdoor and grinned. "What's the holdup?" he asked her as she finally stepped out of the truck.

Chapter 12

On the streets of New York, Nigel thought the lights had gone out. A paint can from the garbage truck was stuck on his head.

"We're over here, Nigel," Samson said, watching the koala stumble into a wall.

"Right!" came Nigel's muffled voice from inside the paint can. "I'll be there in a minute."

The group took a few steps into Times Square. It was still early morning and the streets were empty. "Okay, think," Samson said to his crew. "What'd Benny say? Couple lefts, couple rights!"

Bridget craned her long neck up and looked around. "Bridget, you see the green lady?" Samson asked hopefully.

"I'm looking, I'm looking," Bridget answered, "but I can't see over anything . . . for a change."

Nigel was still trying to find his friends. "How far away are you?" he called as he kept hitting lampposts.

"You in a different continent?"

He finally grabbed hold of something alive. "Is that you, Larry?" he asked, rubbing up against Samson's leg. "You're a very furry snake."

Samson looked down and popped the paint can off Nigel's head with a big claw.

"Guys," Samson said to them as they huddled on the sidewalk, "we don't want to draw attention to ourselves."

From down an alley, there suddenly came the sound of ferocious barking.

"Oh, dogs," Bridget said, relieved. "This should be fun for you, Samson." If Samson could handle a herd of crazed wildebeests, Bridget figured, some yappy dogs would be morning exercise for the huge lion.

But Samson had never faced anything wilder than a family of tourists from Florida. "Nigel, grab Bridget!" Samson said quickly.

"What?" Bridget asked, confused.

"RUN!" Samson shouted as three dogs came tearing down the street.

Nigel howled and clung to Bridget's leg. Larry wrapped himself around her neck, and the whole gang took off through Times Square.

"Not to nitpick," Bridget shouted at Samson as

they ran, "but shouldn't you be tearing them to shreds?"

"All part of the plan," Samson said, guiding them down a side street. "This maneuver's known as the Serengeti Slip." As the dogs raced past the alley, Samson let out a sigh of relief.

Nigel shook his fist in the air. "Go on, you mutts!" he shouted. "We could've taken you!"

The dogs suddenly appeared in the alley.

"Taken you to a . . . disco!" Nigel said, grinning at the snarling dogs. The frightened koala thought a demonstration might help. He shook his hips and danced in a circle, but the dogs were not impressed.

"Larry," Nigel said nervously, "improvise!"

Larry uncoiled and began to bark furiously. The dogs barked more and more loudly. "Larry, that's not helping," Nigel said.

Larry nodded agreeably. "Okay."

The dogs chased the friends down the alley until they reached a dead end. The friends turned their backs to the wall.

"Oh, you dogs think you got bark?" Bridget yelled fearlessly. "Well, Samson's got roar!" She turned her big eyes to Samson. "Show 'em, Sam," she said confidently.

Samson took a huge breath. "Dig deep," he said to himself as the dogs snarled. He had to protect his crew. "You're a lion."

But he couldn't convince himself. *You're no lion,* he thought as the dogs moved closer. He looked for another way out.

A sewer grate was on the ground and a steel beam was overhead. Samson got an idea. "Larry, coil!" he shouted, pointing at the grate.

Larry flicked his tail in a salute and coiled it into the grate. "Check!" he said.

Then Samson looked at Bridget's rump and gave it a pinch. "Sam!" exclaimed Bridget as she bucked and kicked Larry over the steel beam. The grate popped off the manhole, but Bridget was shocked.

Samson saw her expression and said, "I improvised. Now, jump!"

Bridget looked into the black hole. "Down there?"

"Yes!" Samson said as the dogs broke into an attack and tore down the alley. Nigel and Bridget dropped down the hole.

"We're leaving, Larry!" Samson yelled, but Larry couldn't uncoil fast enough. Samson yanked him down into the hole, then jumped in and closed the grate behind them.

Chapter 13

The dogs' snouts slammed into the grate as Larry, Nigel, Bridget, and Samson plunged into total darkness. Nigel's plastic torch provided just enough light for them to keep from stepping on each other.

"Teensy question, Samson," Bridget said. "With those dogs up there, why didn't you just . . . do what you used to do in the Wild? Lionize 'em?"

"I don't have time," Samson said as they slowly crept through the tunnel. "I have to find Ryan."

Larry uncoiled to see a large pool at the end of the tunnel. "What is this spooky place?" he asked, his voice echoing through the damp air.

Samson had no idea where they were. The pool was surrounded by tunnels that went off in every direction. "It, uh, appears to be a human bathing area," he told the gang.

"You mean humans don't lick themselves clean?" Nigel asked, looking at the murky pond. "Disgusting!"

Nigel's liberty torch began to flicker. "No hurry,"

he said to Samson, "but is there a plan?"

"Of course there's a plan," Samson said as he looked at the tunnels. "We follow this water to the big water and then find the lady with the—" But before he could finish, a low growl filled the huge cave.

Bridget was frightened. "Larry, either your stomach is growling or something in your stomach is growling."

"That wasn't me," Larry said quietly.

Nigel stood with his back to the pool, his torch raised in his short right arm like the real Statue of Liberty. Suddenly, everyone was staring at him wide-eyed in terror.

"What?" Nigel said, looking from side to side. Then he heard a splash and took a look over his shoulder. Two huge alligators were slowly rising from the pool.

Larry coiled into a knot as Bridget gasped and took a step back. "So . . . the urban legend is true," Bridget said, referring to the story of pet alligators being flushed away by New Yorkers who could no longer raise them in apartments.

Samson stood tall as the two green alligators lumbered toward them. Larry, Nigel, and Bridget cringed in horror as they grouped tightly behind Samson.

One of the alligators slowly opened his huge mouth. A sound like an enormous burp came out. "I'm gonna say, it looks like you and your crew here are a little far from your borough."

"We're going to the big water," Samson told them. "Nigel, show them what we're looking for."

Nigel nervously stepped forward and struck his best Statue of Liberty pose.

"Nigel," Bridget whispered, nodding toward his torch, "I think it's in her right hand."

Nigel shot Bridget a look and readjusted his torch.

"No idea what he's talkin' about," Stan the alligator said in his New York accent. "You?" he asked his buddy, Carmine.

Big Carmine shook his enormous head, splashing water on Nigel and Samson. "Doesn't even register," he said as his eyes narrowed at the koala.

"You're battin' zero, kid," Stan said.

"Nigel," Samson said quickly. He put his big paw over his head. "Do the thing with the . . . ," and he pointed to Nigel's head.

Nigel rolled his eyes and stuck his claws above his head to make a crown.

The alligators' expressions suddenly changed. "Ah, the big female with the spikes on her melon!"

Carmine said, smiling at Stan. The two nodded. "They're tourists!

"All right, tourists," Carmine said excitedly, "listen up! Ya gotta get to Battery Park. First ya take the Broadway culvert—"

"Whoa! You're sending them down the Broadway culvert?" Stan interjected.

"Yeah, what's wrong with that?"

The two alligators stood on their hind legs to discuss the problem. "They'll get lost at the sewage-treatment plant," Stan told Carmine. "You're sending 'em the wrong way!"

"Nah, get outta here," Carmine argued. "The Wall Street culvert is blocked with construction!"

Stan nodded. "That is true."

"Look, guys, you gonna help or not?" Samson asked finally.

Carmine smiled, showing his huge teeth. "Yeah, sure, of course we're gonna help yas. We're one big family, right? Except for that guy over there," he said, nodding at Nigel. "He scares the—"

Stan banged Carmine on the head. "You done running your mouth yet, Carmine? Huh? Are ya? Huh?

"I apologize. He never got over being flushed down the toilet," Stan said to Samson. He banged

Carmine's head again. "Huh?" he asked the dazed alligator.

"Yeah," Carmine answered, his tongue hanging from the side of his mouth.

"Now, follow me," Stan said to Samson, "because you four won't last ten minutes in this neighborhood. It's a jungle down here."

Samson and his group followed the alligators into one of the dark tunnels.

"Stan!" Carmine suddenly growled. "You know who that is?"

"No," Stan answered.

"That's one of them talking kawana bears!" Carmine said excitedly.

"Oh! 'I'm so cuddly. I like you,'" Stan said, imitating a Nigel doll. "Yeah, that's funny."

"I've seen a lot of those things floating around down here in the sewer," snorted Carmine.

Chapter 14

Nigel, Bridget, Larry, and Samson emerged from the tunnel just as the sun was rising over Battery Park. Huge cranes were already busy stacking shipping containers on the loading dock as Samson jumped onto a box to get a better view.

"Are we in the right place?" Larry asked hopefully.

Nigel was shivering. "Any place without two hilarious alligators seems a move in the right direction."

"Sam, you see anything up there?" Bridget called.

"I sure do," Samson said, gazing at New York Harbor.

Larry and Nigel held on to Bridget's neck as she jumped up behind Samson. "Well, there she is," gasped Bridget, seeing the Statue of Liberty in the harbor, "just like Hamir said."

"Guys, look," Samson said, "we know the box Ryan's in is green, and it's got to be around here somewhere." His eyes scanned the dock. "I need you to—"

"So you're saying that we should shout out if we

see a box that looks exactly like the ones over there," Larry said, interrupting him. He pointed his tail toward some green boxes on the dock.

Samson saw a ship with ZOO TO AFRICA RESCUE on it, just like there had been on the truck that had taken Ryan away. "It hasn't left yet!" he said excitedly. "We can make it. Let's go!"

Samson, Larry, Nigel, and Bridget ran down to the dock through a maze of containers, dodging forklifts and moving crane lines. Out of breath, they arrived at the ship.

Samson heaved a sigh of relief. Nothing was being loaded off the dock at that moment. They stepped up to the railing when suddenly the ship's lines were cast off. It was moving!

Even though it was only feet away, Samson could not reach the towering ship. "No! No!" he yelled, leaning out over the water. "Ryan's on that thing! We've got to stop it!"

Larry coiled around him and pulled him back. "No, Sammy, you'll drown!"

"I've failed. Again," Samson said, dropping from the rail.

Nigel wrinkled his forehead. "I only count one failure," he said. "It's big, but it's just one."

"Good-bye, Ryan," Larry said, waving his tail. "We're gonna miss you."

Samson hung his head when suddenly the sound of an engine *vrooooom*ed beneath the dock. Larry, Bridget, and Nigel lurched to one side as the boards under their feet began to move. "What on earth is going on?" Nigel shouted.

Bridget craned her long neck and saw a man holding a wheel at the other end of the dock. "It's a human," she told the others, "and I don't think he works for the zoo."

Samson suddenly realized that they weren't at the railing of a dock at all. It was the railing of a boat, and the boat was moving them even farther away from Ryan's ship!

"Perhaps now is a good time to . . . improvise?" Nigel suggested to Samson.

Samson wasn't sure what Nigel meant, but Bridget was. She stepped on Samson's tail so hard, he let out a huge *rrrroooooar!*

The captain dove into the harbor, screaming.

"Great . . . one problem down," Nigel said brightly, then looked at the wheel of the ship spinning out of control.

Larry looked at the wheel, too, hypnotized. "Far

out!" he said, jabbing the tip of his tail into it as if he were poking a fan. Suddenly, Larry's tail was caught in the wheel, and—*whoosh*—his entire body was swept into it.

"One disaster to go!" Nigel sighed as Larry's head bonked on the wheel handles.

"Help. Help. Help. Help. Help," Larry cried as his head hit the throttle and the boat began to move faster. It was heading for a large ocean liner!

"Larry, what're you doing?" Samson hollered.

"How do we steer?" Bridget said in a panic. "Who knows how to steer?"

She suddenly realized the answer. "None of us! We're animals!" she wailed.

Samson struggled to pull Larry off, but as he grabbed the snake, he noticed that the boat was turning.

"Aaaaagh!" Nigel screamed as the huge steel hull went by.

"Hey, I think I've got it!" Samson said, taking the wheel in both paws.

He turned the boat, missing the ocean liner by inches.

When they were finally in the clear, the little koala took a deep breath. "Well, that was easy," Nigel said, panting as he looked up at Bridget.

"This isn't so difficult," Samson said, smiling as he stood at the helm. "I'm the lion of the sea! Arrgh!"

"Well done, sir," Nigel said with a salute. "Captain of our team and now captain of this vessel!"

"Um, I hate to be Miss Negative," Bridget said, "but in all this melee, we seem to have lost Ryan's boat."

The team looked around in confusion.

Bridget looked out to the empty horizon. "Nothing," she said. "He's gone."

Chapter 15

But somewhere over the Atlantic, a determined squirrel was riding on the back of a Canadian goose.

"There, Nelson!" Benny exclaimed, pointing at the cargo ship. "The green boxes!

"And there's my buddies!" Benny said excitedly as he spotted the boat with Bridget's long neck leaning over the side. "And my love!" he shouted. "Let's go in!"

Nelson led the V formation of geese behind him into a dive. "Aaaagh!" Benny yelled, clutching Nelson's neck.

At the same time, aboard the boat, Samson and his friends were trying to figure out which way to go. "We'll head away from the sun," Samson decided.

"No," Nigel said, walking in a circle. "Towards the sun. To the north! Starboard, or . . . leftboard! Just follow my finger!" the flustered little koala argued.

"Oh, please!" Bridget huffed. "You guys wouldn't

know the answer if it fell from the sky and hit you in the head!" Suddenly, Larry noticed a blur of flapping wings behind Bridget.

"Whoa! Whoa! Whoa!" Benny yelled as Nelson the goose crashed into Bridget.

Benny hung on to Bridget as she screamed, "Is it a bat? It's a bat! Get it off me! Get it off me!"

She shook her head, flinging Benny to the deck.

"Benny!" she exclaimed, looking down at the winded squirrel.

"Geese!" Larry said excitedly as the rest of Nelson's flock landed.

"Are you all right?" Bridget asked.

Benny sighed. "Yes, my princess."

"Benny, you made it!" Samson said to the dizzy squirrel.

"You're my best friend," Benny said, rubbing his head. "Best friends should stick together. Even not-so-best friends who knock you off a speeding garbage truck," he said, glaring at the others.

"Excuse me, but I begged them to go back and get you," Nigel said, fibbing. "Just so you know."

Samson rolled his eyes. "Benny, could you see Ryan's boat from up there?"

Benny smiled. "Well, it just so happens I could see

it. And," he said confidently, "we're in luck." He pointed to Nelson. "Canadian geese," he said proudly. "Experts at intercontinental travel."

"How's it goin', eh?" honked Nelson.

Nigel curiously approached the goose. "Hey, birdie, is it true Canada has lax immigration policies for koalas?"

"I'll take it from here, Nige," Samson said, stepping up to the geese. "My son's out there. We really need your help. Can you lead us to that boat?"

"No problem, eh, just follow us and Bob's your uncle!" Nelson said brightly. Nigel, Larry, and Bridget nodded enthusiastically, thinking that that must be Canadian for yes.

The geese flew up into an arrow formation, with Nelson in the lead. "Try not to lag too far behind, eh?" Nelson called back.

Samson was thrilled. For the first time since they'd left the zoo, he felt there was a real chance to find Ryan.

"Hey, Benny," Samson said, smiling at his old friend, "thanks." Benny gave Samson a tiny thumbs-up.

"And FYI," Samson added, "Bridget was very concerned when you fell off the truck."

Benny swaggered over to the tall giraffe. "Betcha

didn't know I could ride geese, did you?" he asked her, then added with a gleam in his eye, "Bareback."

Bridget felt her stomach turn. "Oh, brother," she said, leaning her head over the side of the boat.

"Sammy," Larry asked, "are we going to the Wild now?"

Samson steered the boat behind the geese and smiled. "I think we are, Larry."

Chapter 16

With Samson at the wheel, the boat sailed through high seas and treacherous storms. But as the days passed, the heat became unbearable.

"I can't take it anymore!" Nigel moaned as he looked into the blinding sun.

He waved his little fist at the sky. "He's taunting us!" he said. "Stop laughing at us, you solar twit!"

He looked at Samson. "Captain Bligh, sir, are the ice cream cones ready? The crew, they're on the verge of mutiny!"

"Nigel, please," Benny said, hoping the crazed koala would snap out of it. Too many days of bright sunshine and not enough to eat had made the koala delirious.

But Nigel was not comforted. "If you don't give us ice creams pretty quick, you're gonna walk the plank, sir!"

"Nigel . . . ," Samson said.

"I don't care if I drown," Nigel said, bumping

around the deck. "I'm getting off this death cruise right now." Samson was about to grab Nigel by the back of the neck when the boat suddenly hit something with a *thwump*.

The exhausted crew toppled over, Bridget landing right on top of Nigel.

"Captain Bligh," Nigel cried, "we hit an iceberg!"

He struggled out from under Bridget. "Permission to go down with the ship!" Nigel yelled, jumping overboard.

The gang rushed to the boat's railing. They were stunned to see Nigel belly flopped on a sandy beach.

The little crew had beached themselves on the shore of a tropical island.

"Whoa . . . ," Bridget said, seeing a dense, dark jungle in the distance. She turned to Samson. "It must feel like a lifetime since you've been here."

Samson gulped as he looked at the Wild for the first time. "Yeah," he said, exchanging looks with Benny, "a lifetime."

Chapter 17

Nigel was still a little dazed as the nervous crew carefully made their way to a loading dock on the beach. A crane was moving the green boxes from the big ship that had come all the way from New York.

"Oh, will you look at that!" Larry said. "They're releasing the green boxes back into the Wild."

Benny climbed onto Bridget's head to get a better look. Dozens of animals were being held in a huge pen. "Guys," Benny said, "they're putting animals *inside* the green boxes."

Samson could see that Benny was right. The animals were being herded from the holding pen into the containers. "I just can't figure out why," Benny said to Samson.

Nigel raised his paw with an idea. "It's a tunnel to another dimension," he mumbled. "Can't you see?"

Bridget gave Nigel a look. "Uh, Sam? Who is this guy?"

But Nigel kept blathering. "They go in; they come

The New York Zoo gets wild after dark.

Samson the Wild is the leader of the zoo.

Benny wants the candy bracelet
for his girlfriend, Bridget.

At the championship game,
Samson pulls out the secret play.

Samson gets to the fence just as
Ryan's truck is pulling away.

Nigel and Samson are awestruck by the big city.

Nigel admires his new outfit.

They've reached the Wild at last!

Bridget, Larry, and Nigel cannot believe
that Samson isn't really from the Wild.

Ryan wants to fight the wildebeests,
but Samson tells him to run.

Samson finally tells Ryan the truth.

Ryan is surprised that his father
is not from the Wild.

Benny tells Samson that his friends need him.

The wildebeests bow to their new leader.

Nigel meets the Omen, an old stuffed koala.

Blag and the wildebeests leave Kazar.
They are tired of following his orders.

out somewhere else."

"It's all right, Nigel," Samson said. He was patting the little koala on the head when suddenly the ground began to rumble. A puff of smoke rose from a mountain in the jungle.

"Hey, you think it has anything to do with that?" Larry asked, pointing his tail at the volcano.

Bridget heaved a sigh. "Either I'm starving or Larry is making sense," she said.

Samson knew it was true: a volcano was erupting, and the animals were being taken off the island to safety.

"Larry's right," Samson said as he saw two elephants being loaded into a box. "Those animals are being rescued."

Chapter 18

At that moment, Ryan could feel his green box rising off the deck of the ship. The crane's cable slipped, and in an instant, Ryan's box dropped to the ground.

The fall made the box crack open. Ryan pushed on the door with all his might. He could hear the ship's crew yelling, "Hey, look out for that lion!" as he bolted from the box.

The cub ran so quickly, he frightened the other animals who were waiting to board the ship. An elephant reared back and trumpeted, causing even more chaos.

Samson and his crew turned from the volcano to see Ryan running toward the jungle.

"Ryan!" Samson shouted, running after his son, but Ryan couldn't hear him over the confusion in the loading area.

"Oh, no," Samson gasped as Ryan disappeared into the jungle.

"RYAN!" he called. The big lion ran so fast, he hardly noticed that he'd run through a wall of trees and into the wild jungle.

The darkness of the dense jungle surrounded Samson, and there was no sign of Ryan anywhere.

Benny suddenly appeared at his side. "I can't believe it!" Samson said to him. "I was so close! He was right there! We'll never find him now! Do you know how big it is out there?"

But Benny wasn't about to let his friend give up now. "Will you get a hold of yourself?" he said, giving Samson a smack on the nose. "Use your instincts," he added under his breath.

Samson rubbed his stinging snout just as Bridget, with Larry and Nigel on her neck, stumbled into the jungle.

Nigel was still undone. "I don't want to run anymore," he gasped.

"Don't worry," Benny said confidently. "Everything's under control."

Suddenly, Samson raised his head. "I got it! I got Ryan's scent!" he exclaimed. The huge lion tore down the path.

"He got it?" Benny said in shock. "I mean, he got it! He got it! Let's go!"

"Hooray!" Larry cried.

"Wait for us!" Bridget called, high-stepping over the jungle vines.

"Ah," Nigel moaned as he was slapped in the face by a long green vine. "I'm not designed for this. I want a car!"

Chapter 19

Samson rushed toward the scent. "Hey, guys," he called, lifting a small shrub, "I found him!" But Samson came face to face with a furry round rodent squatting on a hollow stump.

"Doesn't anybody knock anymore?" the hyrax asked, unhappy about the intrusion.

"Where's my son?" Samson asked, embarrassed. "Did he come through here?"

"Yeah, now that I think of it, he did come through here," the smelly little hyrax said. He looked into the hollow log he was using as his bathroom. "Hello, come on up, baby lion," he called, sticking his head in the hole. "Your dad's here. Well, what do you know, there's a whole pride of lions down here!" he said sarcastically.

Samson hung his head as his little crew ran to catch up with him.

"Um," Bridget said, looking at the hyrax, "I was under the impression you had Ryan's scent."

"I, uh, had Ryan's scent," Samson said, trying to cover his blunder, "but, uh, my predator instincts must've kicked in since, you know, I haven't eaten for a while."

"Exactly!" Benny said, quickly giving Samson a pat on the back. "You never know when those predator instincts are gonna kick in."

Nigel suddenly brightened. "Excellent! We get to see the legend in action!"

Samson wanted nothing more than to find Ryan, get out of there, and be back in his zoo home. "I'd love to," he told them, "but we just don't have time. . . ."

"Oh, ho, we've got the time, Sammy!" Nigel said excitedly as he picked up the little hyrax and started slapping him silly.

"Oh, I can't bear to watch!" Bridget said, closing her huge eyes. "But I have to!" she added, opening just one.

Samson looked at the hyrax, who was waiting to die. He picked the hyrax up, raised him to his mouth, and said, "Go on, get out of here." Samson let the little hyrax go and lowered his head.

"The legend just dropped his dinner," Bridget said in shock.

"Oh, boy," Benny said nervously. He knew that

Samson was going to have some explaining to do.

The hyrax brushed himself off and glared at Samson. "What's wrong? I'm not good enough for you to eat or something?"

"No, it's just that I'm allergic to nuts," Samson said, making the hyrax furious.

"Oh, now I get it," the hyrax said, boldly taking a step toward Samson. "You're going to toy with me? Beat me up a little, then pounce just when I get my hopes up? How exciting!"

"C'mon, guys," Samson said, turning his back on the angry rodent. "Ryan can't be far."

"Hey! I'm not finished with you!" the hyrax shouted. "I am a delicacy. My flesh has fruity woodnotes!"

"Watch it, you little hors d'oeuvre," Larry said. "That's Samson the Wild you're talking to."

The hyrax laughed. "You call this wild? This is a cat. A big fat tame pussycat!"

"Okay, that's enough!" Samson snarled.

"Ooh, the pussycat hissed at me," the hyrax said, imitating Samson's growl. "Maybe I should hide behind the koala for protection! And while we're at it, could you slap me in the face a few times?"

"Ignore him, Nigel," Samson said, fuming.

"Don't bother. I'm leaving!" the hyrax said as he stomped into the bushes.

"Run for your lives, everyone!" the grumpy rodent yelled. "It's a lion with moral issues!"

Samson and his crew watched as the hyrax ran off and smashed into a bush. "And I've had it with you, too!" the angry hyrax shouted as he throttled the bush with all his might.

Chapter 20

Bridget finally broke the silence. "That hyrax back there . . . It was sort of like you . . . couldn't eat him," she said gently.

Larry and Nigel nodded in agreement. "And what about those dogs in the alley?" Nigel asked. "There was no munching there, either."

"Samson, if I didn't know any better," Larry said, "I'd almost say that you're . . ."

"A vegetarian?" Benny offered hopefully.

Larry shook his head. "No, that's not what I was gonna say."

But everyone knew what Larry meant.

Nigel said, "You were gonna say that it's almost like he's not from . . ."

"The Wild?" Samson asked sheepishly. "Well, you're right!" he said. He was tired of living a lie. "I'm not from the Wild! I'm a fraud, okay? I'm a liar."

Samson saw their disappointed expressions.

"I can't protect you out here. I'm sorry. Just go back to the boat. I've got to go find my son," he said, and ran off alone.

"Benny, please tell me we're not in a jungle with an eight-inch squirrel protecting us," said Bridget.

"Actually, I'm nine inches," shot back the brave squirrel.

Nigel also realized that he was lost in the jungle without a brave lion to protect him. "WE ARE GOING TO DIE!" he screamed.

Bridget and Larry joined Nigel as he ran in circles screaming, "Aaaaghh! Aaaarrghhh! Eeeeehhhh!"

"Hey, guys," Benny yelled. "Will the three of you calm down already?" He let out a whistle rarely heard outside New York City, and the trio froze.

"How could he lie to us?" Bridget wailed.

"We're his best friends," Nigel said sadly.

"Maybe he lied because he didn't want to tell us the truth," Larry said, nodding.

Bridget was ready to give up. "Okay, whatever. Let's just go back to the boat!"

They started walking away.

"Wait, wait, where you going?" Benny asked them. He knew that if there was ever a time Samson needed their help, it was now. But Nigel, Larry, and Bridget ignored him.

"Stop!" Benny pleaded. Then he said, "Bridget, if you go . . . I'm, uh, I'm breaking up with you."

Benny knew that Bridget would stop just to argue with him.

The giraffe dug her hooves into the ground. "We were never going out in the first place," she huffed, looking down at the ridiculously small squirrel.

Benny jumped on the opportunity. "Listen," he told them, "I know you're scared. But at least we've got each other. Sammy's got nobody."

Nigel, Larry, and Bridget looked at each other, then into the forbidding jungle. "He's out there all alone, and so is Ryan," Benny said.

Chapter 21

As Larry rode on Bridget's back, Benny bravely led the way through the jungle. Determined to find their friends, Nigel stoutly brought up the rear.

"Ryan? Ryan?" Larry called softly as the jungle closed in around them.

"Sammy! Sammy!" Benny shouted.

Bridget raised her long legs, trying to step over the thick undergrowth. "I wasn't meant for the Wild," she said. "I was made to nibble and be elegant and appear in children's books as the letter G."

"Come on," Nigel said breezily, "this isn't scary, is it? It's just leaves and vines and . . ." The little koala suddenly gasped as he looked down. "Aggh!" he screamed until he realized that he was looking at his own paw. "Oh, that's my foot," he said cheerily.

"Nigel, keep a lookout back there," Benny ordered. "You too, Larry.

"Nigel?" Benny called out. "I gave you an order.

Would a little 'Sir, yes, sir!' kill you?"

Benny turned around. "Nigel?" he repeated, but there was no answer. "Okay, that's not funny, Nigel," Benny said, but the little koala was nowhere in sight. The entire group froze.

"He's gone!" Larry howled. "Oh, no! We're doomed! First Ryan, then Samson, now Nigel . . . I do believe in zoos, I do, I do, I do believe in zoos. . . ."

He sprung onto Bridget's neck. "Larry, you're tensing up!" Bridget coughed as he coiled more and more tightly. "Think calm thoughts!"

"Don't panic," Benny said, trying to reassure everyone. "I'm in charge here."

"That's why we're panicking!" said Bridget.

Benny needed a plan. "I say we fan out in circles!" he decided.

"What're we, peacocks?" Bridget hollered. "We don't fan; we run. RUN FOR YOUR LIVES, EVERY-ONE!"

"Guys," Larry said, looking over Bridget's shoulder, "I've got an idea." He pointed his tail at a group of wildebeests that now stood in their path. "Why don't we ask them?"

The leaves of the jungle rustled as more of the large gray herd surrounded them. The beasts had leathery skin and their horns were sharp.

"It's okay," Benny said nervously. "They have hooves, which means they don't hunt; they graze."

Blag, a large wildebeest, began to growl.

"But they're licking their chops!" Bridget said in shock.

"I'll take the one with the funny knees," Blag said, eyeing Bridget.

"The funny knees!" Benny exclaimed. The insult to his true love sent him into a rage. He grabbed a twig and charged at the snarling wildebeest.

"Benny, no!" Bridget cried as Blag lowered his huge head and tossed Benny against a rock with a flick of his horn.

Benny fell to the ground, unconscious. "Benny?" Bridget said, rushing to his side.

Blag nodded toward Bridget and Larry. "Get them," he ordered with a vicious smile.

Chapter 22

Later, in another part of the jungle, little Nigel was returning to consciousness. "Just back off," he mumbled, still dreaming. "I'm sorry, I'm not that kind of koala bear."

Nigel couldn't understand why he was bouncing along through the jungle. Then he remembered. "Ah, right," he said to himself, then leaned forward on the two horns that curled around him. He looked into Blag's beady black eyes.

"'Scuse me. Hello," Nigel said politely. "Terribly sorry to bother you. Um, do you speak koala? Sprechen Sie koala?" he tried.

But Blag only grunted.

"Right, could you possibly not go towards the big smoking thing?" Nigel asked as the wildebeests marched through the rocky entrance of the smoking volcano. They began to chant as Nigel got closer.

"G'day, mate! G'day, mate! G'day, mate! G'day, mate!" the wildebeests said over and over. Nigel could see the shadows of the great beasts against the cave walls inside the towering volcano. They were on their hind legs, doing spins and flips.

"What a strange place for a party," Nigel said, still riding on Blag's horns.

Three hundred dancing, spinning wildebeests suddenly stopped when the koala applauded. They faced him, as if they were waiting for him to say something."Very good, very organized," he said to the herd, hoping to calm them down.

But his strategy didn't work. The wildebeests started again, whirling faster and faster, chanting, "Really nice day, really nice day, really nice day," to the astounded koala.

As Blag carried Nigel through the crowd and into a chamber of the volcano, the wildebeests got wilder.

"They're frighteningly horrible monster-beasts!" Nigel gulped. "But they're not bad dancers."

In perfect sequence, the grotesque beasts did a complicated dance routine for Nigel to the tune of "I'm so cuddly. I like you!" from the zoo's stuffed koala toy.

Only Blag had trouble keeping up with the light-footed beasts. He whispered the steps out loud: "Step-kick, pivot-kick, walk, walk, walk." But it was no use. He just couldn't keep up with the speedy dance number.

Finally, Blag tripped, throwing Nigel high in the air. Blag caught him just as he was about to land on top of a huge flight of stone steps.

Chapter 23

*S*nooooooort. An even more hideous wildebeest stepped out from the shadows and greeted Nigel.

"AAAGHH!" Nigel screamed as he looked at its scarred face. "What is that?"

"I am Kazar," the wildebeest answered. "Leader. Prophet. Choreographer. And with your help . . . carnivore!"

The little koala put his paws over his eyes as Blag gently lifted him up and set him down. "Don't kill me," he begged. "I've had such a weird life. It's not fair!"

Nigel peeked out for a second, and he was amazed. He was sitting on a throne, and on the wall in front of him was a carving of a giant warrior koala. When he gazed before him, he saw the entire wildebeest nation bowing down to him.

Nigel sat up. "Oh, I get it," he said brightly, "a yoga retreat!"

At the same time, Samson, off in the jungle alone, was still hoping that his instincts could lead him to Ryan. He shouted the cub's name over and over, but there was no answer.

The big lion wandered through the dense undergrowth. Every place he looked in seemed dark and mysterious. "Come on. You can do this," Samson was saying to himself when he suddenly heard whispers.

"Follow your instincts. . . . Follow your instincts," the small voices were saying. Samson quickly spun around. The whispering stopped, but Samson noticed a patch of leaves on the ground turn polka-dotted!

He moved his nose toward the leaves when— *ping!*—the polka dots disappeared.

Samson jumped back, then saw that farther ahead the trunk of a tree had turned candy striped!

Mystified, Samson walked toward the tree. As the stripes disappeared, he could see that another tree ahead had turned completely plaid! He thought he heard voices calling him forward, and he followed.

Not far away, high in the trees, two vultures named Scab and Scraw were scouting Ryan.

"A lion cub!" Scab whispered to his

leathery-headed friend.

The two took off and headed for the volcano. "We must tell Kazar!" Scraw said excitedly.

"Five bones says that thing blows before sundown," cackled Scab as the two messengers flew toward the bubbling volcano.

Chapter 24

Inside the volcano, Nigel was still sitting on his throne. He spoke politely to the wildebeests as they bowed to him. "Um, thank you very much," he said, still a little nervous, "but I'm afraid I've got to run. Koalas are very busy bees. So if you could just buzz me toward the door . . ."

Kazar stepped forward. "For centuries, we've watched our brethren perish at the claw of the lion. Today, we put our hoof down. No longer will we dwell at the bottom of the food chain."

Nigel nodded, not knowing what the heck this wildebeest was talking about. "Well, yes," he said, trying to be agreeable. "I should say so."

"There were those who doubted that you'd arrive to lead us," Kazar went on. "But I always believed in the Omen."

"Ah, the Omen. Right," Nigel said, trying to follow along. "Remind me again?"

Kazar motioned to a group of wildebeests, who

moved to the side, revealing an *I Like You* Nigel doll on a pedestal. It was the same doll sold at the zoo gift shop. Nigel was shocked. "Yoooouuuu!" he yelled at the doll.

"Sent down by the gods years ago," Kazar said.

Nigel slumped in his throne and listened, dumbstruck, as Kazar explained that this very plush toy had fallen out of a plane many years ago. When it had fallen, hitting a lion on the head and scaring it away, the doll had saved the young Kazar from being eaten on the spot. Who knew that that young wildebeest would one day grow up to be the king of all wildebeests . . . forever worshipping the image of the koala?

"Oh, Great Him, you must lead us in our transformation from prey to predator," pleaded Kazar.

Nigel thought for a moment. "I am the Great Him?" he asked, making sure he was getting it right. "The Great . . ." He walked over to the stuffed doll. "Him?" he asked, pointing at it.

The wildebeests nodded.

"So this is all your fault!" Nigel said, lunging at the stuffed toy.

Chapter 25

Nigel's coronation was interrupted when two vultures flapped into the cave screaming, "Kazar!"

The great wildebeest pinned one of them to the cave wall. "How dare you interrupt my audience with the Great Him!" Kazar growled.

"But we found a lion cub!" Scab gasped.

Kazar froze. "You did?"

Nigel's ears stood straight up at the word *lion*.

"Was he a big lion?" Nigel asked them. "Big hair . . . well, a mullet, really . . ."

Kazar turned to Nigel, overjoyed. "Great Him, you've brought two lions with you?"

Nigel nodded. "Like any Great Him, I travel with an entourage."

"Worry not, Your Himness," Kazar said, bowing. "I shall have Blag bring the lions here. And he'd better not screw this up like he screwed up my dance number!" He shot Blag a look.

"I lost count for one verse." Blag shrugged.

Kazar demonstrated the dance. "Step-kick, pivot-kick, walk, walk, walk!" he shouted at Blag.

"Ahhh, why do we even bother rehearsing?" Kazar said to Nigel. "A good chorus line is so hard to put together."

Nigel nodded and raised one of his furry eyebrows, a bit surprised by Kazar's interest in dance—and his attitude toward his pupils.

Kazar turned to the vultures. "Take to the skies!" he yelled. Then, turning to Blag, he shouted, "Find them! Bring us those lions!"

Blag left the cave with five other wildebeests. Scab and Scraw were flying above them.

Nigel was nodding enthusiastically about the search when the volcano suddenly began to rumble. The herd looked at Nigel in awe.

"The gods celebrate the fulfillment of our destiny! We stamp our hooves in praise of the Great Him!" Kazar said solemnly.

"Holy moly," Nigel said, afraid the whole mountain was about to come down.

The wildebeests immediately started chanting, "Holy moly! Holy moly! Holy moly! You are our king!"

Nigel smiled. He was beginning to like the sound

of the word *king*. He let out a laugh that echoed through the cave.

Bridget and Larry were being held prisoner in another part of the cave. They were surrounded by snarling wildebeest guards, and the ground was shaking.

"Does anyone happen to have a Richter scale on them?" Bridget said nervously. "This is a bit of an unprecedented feeling, but I actually wish Benny were here."

"Okay, I've got a plan," Larry said, trying to make her feel better. "You kick one of them; I'll swallow one of them. That leaves . . ." Larry thought for a second. ". . . four, five . . . about sixty-four more."

Bridget's shoulders dropped. "It's official," she moaned. "We're doomed!"

Chapter 26

The shadows of the two vultures passed over the jungle as Samson, far below, continued to search for Ryan. Samson didn't see the vultures overhead. All his attention was focused on following the bushes and rocks as they changed color, leading him deeper and deeper into the jungle.

He ran from plaid palms to purple-polka-dotted ferns, then on to blue-striped tree bark. His instincts told him he was being led in the right direction, right to Ryan. But Samson didn't know that the vultures flying above him were heading straight for Ryan, too. And sadly, they found Ryan first.

The vultures spotted Ryan trying to hide high in a tree. In the blink of an eye, Scab and Scraw swirled down and began dive-bombing him from all angles.

Ryan was swiping a paw at the flapping black wings when the branch he was standing on suddenly snapped. He tumbled to the ground, where a tree limb pinned him. Scab and Scraw were delighted.

The vultures landed with a bounce and carefully approached the cub. When they were sure he was helpless, Scraw leaned in and took a peck.

"Ow!" Ryan yelled, and let out a scratchy roar.

Scraw and Scab laughed at his weak roar and closed in on the little lion, pecking wildly.

"Aaaaagh!" Ryan screamed as he tried to fight them off.

Not far away, Samson raised his head. "Ryan?" he called out.

Samson ran faster as he heard his son yelling, "Help!"

Scraw and Scab saw the racing lion crashing through the underbrush, and each took off like a shot.

Samson rushed to Ryan's side. "Ryan! Oh, Ryan! I can't believe it! I found you! Are you all right?" he asked, taking his son in his arms. "Are you hurt?" He hugged Ryan close.

Ryan was breathless. "Dad, I got trapped in this crate and I escaped and ran into the jungle, and I heard these vultures and they wanted to kill me. You wouldn't have been scared, but—"

"Ryan . . . ," Samson said, interrupting him. "I have to tell you something."

"What?" Ryan asked.

"Shhh . . . ," Samson suddenly whispered.

All at once a group of angry wildebeests charged through the brush. Ryan sprung to his feet.

"Run!" Samson shouted.

"Huh?" Ryan asked, confused.

"RUN!" Samson yelled, giving Ryan a shove. The two ran side by side.

Ryan knew his dad's wildebeest stories well. "Dad, you should be chasing them! Like—like you used to!"

"Those were just stories," Samson responded.

"But now's your chance to show me for real!" Ryan said with excitement.

Samson and Ryan zigzagged through the jungle, the wildebeests keeping up with their every move. "This way!" Samson shouted, heading toward a tree overlooking a cliff.

"Dad, what's going on?" Ryan panted as Samson pushed him up into the tree. Samson climbed up behind him. "They're just a bunch of wimpy donkeys!" declared the cub.

As the wildebeests moved closer, Samson tried to protect his son. "Ryan, shhh . . . ," said Samson.

The wildebeests ran past their tree, and Samson knew that the time to tell his story had finally come.

Chapter 27

"**Y**ou could kick their rumps," Ryan said when they were safe on a high branch.

"RYAN! I can't!" Samson finally admitted. "Those stories aren't true. I can't fight them!"

Ryan looked into his huge father's face.

"What do you mean?" he asked, stunned.

Samson took a breath. It would take all the courage he had to tell his son the truth. "I was young," he began, "still just a cub."

As Samson told his story to Ryan, the memories of being a young circus lion flooded back.

A curtain rose. Behind it was a cage decorated to look like Africa. Inside the circular cage, little Samson sat on a pedestal. He was wearing a fake mane of rope, and his face was smudged with circus paint to make him look mean.

As the spotlight focused on the cage, Samson's father said, "Samson! Swallow that fear and stand tall!" His father was a huge lion, born in the Wild.

"Witness the greatest day in our young lion's life!" the announcer said to the crowd. "The day he discovers his roar!"

Young Samson looked up at his father. "Dad, I can't do it!" he said.

His father glared at him. "Now go!" he growled.

Young Samson stumbled down from the pedestal as his father shook his head.

From across the ring, a mechanical wildebeest suddenly charged at him.

"Listen as Samson unleashes a roar so mighty, it launches this wildebeest clear off the savannah!" the announcer called. The crowd held their breath.

"Samson! Dig deep!" his father barked as the wildebeest barreled down a track and stopped only an inch from Samson's nose.

Young Samson opened his mouth and let out a tiny squeak.

Samson's father turned away, disgusted, as the audience laughed.

"I should have known," the huge lion said. "If you'd been born in the Wild, you'd know how to roar. You're no son of mine."

"Dad! Dad! Dad!" Samson called out to his father. But no one called back. Young Samson was placed in a cage, never to see his father again.

Samson blinked, and he was once again looking into Ryan's eyes. "When they shipped me to the zoo," Samson told Ryan, "I never wanted anyone to know where I came from. Especially those closest to me."

"But all those stories you tell?" asked Ryan in disbelief.

"I should have told you sooner. I'm so sorry, Ryan," Samson said.

Ryan was devastated. "Everything you told me was a lie!" he yelled at his father.

The wildebeests charged the tree.

"Hang on, son!" Samson called out.

Two more wildebeests hit the tree, and Ryan fell to the ground. The tree broke at its trunk and leaned over the cliff, with Samson dangling over the edge.

The wildebeests surrounded Ryan. "Help!" he yelled to his dad as the huge lion fought to climb back onto the cliff.

Ryan tried to reach his dad, but Blag pinned his tail down, stopping him. "Aaagh!" Ryan yelled as the huge tree toppled over the edge of the cliff, taking Samson with it. "Daaad! Help me!"

"RYAN!" Samson shouted as he fell.

Ryan saw his father hit the ground below. "Noooo!" Ryan cried.

Samson could see Ryan's face going in and out of focus before everything went black.

Chapter 28

In the jungle, Benny shook himself awake and rubbed his aching head. He was still lying against the rock where Blag had tossed him in a rage.

The little squirrel stood and swayed. "Bridget! Larry!" he called out, but he was all alone. "They're gone," he said to himself.

Still dizzy, Benny began stumbling through the jungle. *I gotta find them. No, no, I gotta find Samson first! No,* he thought, *first . . .* He stopped and looked around. Samson was lying on a rock just ahead of him. The lion's eyes were closed.

"Sam. Sam!" Benny cried out, running to his friend's side. But Samson didn't move.

Just as poor Benny was losing hope, Ryan's hopes soared. The wildebeests had taken him to the volcano and thrown him in with his two friends. "Bridget! Larry!" Ryan cried. He hadn't seen them since the night of the turtle-curling championship.

"Ryan!" Bridget gasped. "You're alive! You're alive!"

Ryan threw his front paws around Bridget's neck.

"Where's my hug?" Larry said, overjoyed to see the cub. Larry coiled himself around Ryan and gave him a squeeze. "There it is!" the happy snake said.

"Larry," Ryan gasped, "good to see you, too."

He caught his breath as Larry loosened his grip. "What're you guys doing here?"

"We came here with your father," Bridget told him, "to find you."

Larry nodded. "And he's probably out there right now looking for us."

Ryan was choking back tears. "I wish he were," he said to them, "but . . . some of these wildebeests pushed him off a cliff."

"What?" Larry and Bridget said at the same time.

"And I don't think he made it," Ryan said. "I don't see how he could."

"Oh, Ryan," sighed Bridget.

The young cub's head was bowed as he said sadly, "I'm sorry I got you into this."

Chapter 29

Blag and Kazar stood on a ledge above the prisoners. "Kazar, I think you'll be very pleased with what I brought you," Blag said proudly.

Kazar looked over the ledge and saw Ryan. "What's this? Where's the older lion?"

Blag sensed that the great Kazar wasn't as pleased as Blag had hoped he'd be. "Uh . . . well," Blag said, trying to explain, "there was a cliff, and, uh . . . he kinda fell off. . . ."

"That's twice you've been out of step today, Blag!" Kazar bellowed.

Blag took a step back and slipped off the ledge. "Klutz!" Kazar shouted as Blag tried to hang on.

Kazar leaned down. "You know we can't ascend to the top of the food chain until we eat a lion!" Then he looked at Ryan. "Well, at least there'll be enough for my ascension."

"What about the rest of us?" Blag said, struggling.

Kazar shrugged and turned away. "Step. Kick.

Pivot. Kick," he sneered, turning back and kicking Blag in the head.

Blag fell into the holding area with Ryan, Bridget, and Larry. The other wildebeests laughed as he got to his feet. Blag looked at the little gang and told the guards, "Bring the sacrifices to the Great Him!"

Chapter 30

Benny patted his old friend as he tried to hold back tears. "Why did I let him go off by himself?" he said, shaking his head mournfully. "He couldn't catch a cold, much less his own lunch."

"Bet I could catch you," Samson said weakly.

"Please," Benny sniffed. "My natural predator is fuel-injected . . . WHAT?" he said, jumping for joy on Samson's big body. Samson was alive!

"I knew you weren't really gone! I knew it! Come on, I knew it! We're still buddies, right?"

Samson didn't move. "I lost Ryan. There were too many," he said slowly. "They just took him."

"Who took him?" Benny demanded.

"Wildebeests," Samson told him.

"The freaks with the hooves!" Benny exclaimed. "They got Larry and Bridget, too!"

Samson closed his huge eyes. "Couldn't fight . . . couldn't . . . ," the big lion said. Benny sensed that Samson was slipping away again.

"C'mon, Sam," Benny said. "You're a lion! You come from a long line of kings! And yeah, maybe you're not from the Wild, but fighting's in your blood!"

"No. I'll never be a real lion," Samson said.

"Wrong! You are a real lion! It doesn't matter where you're from—zoo, jungle, goldfish bowl. It's what's in here," Benny said, thumping on his little chest, "that determines who you are. At least that's what you always told your son."

Samson raised his head and looked at Benny. "He's out there, Sammy," Benny said, motioning toward the dark jungle. "And he needs you. Who else is gonna teach him how to roar?"

Samson willed himself to stand. "That's it, Sammy, that's it!" he said, to himself. He remembered his father and that sad day at the circus, and he stood taller. Then he shook his mane and raised his chin majestically. "Let's go find my son," he told Benny. "And my friends."

"Yeah!" Benny cheered, throwing a fist into the air. "Nothing's gonna stop us!" Then he looked around. "Except . . . that we have no idea where we're going."

Suddenly, a red and yellow arrow appeared on a fallen log.

A whispering caught their attention. It sounded like voices saying, "Follow your instincts."

"What's that?" Benny asked, confused.

"My . . . uh . . . instincts?" Samson told Benny.

Chapter 31

Benny and Samson followed the changing colors through the jungle. "You're almost there," the little voices whispered as Benny and Samson climbed a blue plaid rock.

"That settles it," Benny said after seeing stripes and polka dots everywhere. "My mother definitely drank pool water when she was pregnant with me."

"Benny, look," Samson whispered as they stood on the plaid rock.

Benny saw two snorting wildebeests guarding the volcano's craggy entrance. "The freaks with hooves!" he said, trying to control his anger.

"Ryan's in there," Samson said, and bolted toward the volcano.

"Whoa, whoa!" Benny said, trying to hold him back. "You can't just barge in. That's suicide!"

"Benny, get out of my—" But before Samson could finish, they were surrounded by whispers.

"Don't listen to the rat," the little voices said.

"Hey, who you calling rat?" Benny asked, looking around. No one was there, but a voice answered, "You!"

"Shhh . . . ," another little voice said, "you'll give away our position!"

The insulted squirrel took a swing toward the voice. He connected and heard it yell, "Owww!"

A chameleon suddenly appeared on a rock, rubbing his head. "I'll have you written up for that," he said to Benny.

From nowhere another little voice shouted, "Fool! You blew our cover! Men, scatter!" Hundreds of chameleons materialized on rocks and trees and began to run.

"Not so fast," Benny snapped, grabbing a chameleon by the neck. "Look who I got, Sammy. It's your lion instincts."

Samson was astounded. "Who are you guys?" he asked.

"Our names aren't important," a chameleon answered.

"I'm Cloak," another chameleon said, nodding. "He's Camo. We're covert agents."

Samson raised his brow. "Why've you been leading me around everywhere?"

"I'm afraid that's classified," Camo told him.

Cloak nodded again. "'Cause the wildebeests have gone mad," he said flatly.

"Cloak!" Camo yelled, socking him.

"What?" Cloak said. "It's not like I told 'em our plan is to use them to defeat Kazar. . . ."

"Listen," Samson said, "just tell me—did they take my son in there?"

Camo shook his head. "That's need-to-know."

Cloak nodded. "They did. And they think the koala's a god."

Camo hit his partner. "You're the worst covert agent ever!" he yelled.

"Oh yeah? Then why can I do this?" Cloak demanded, jumping on Benny and calling for reinforcements.

In an instant, dozens of chameleons jumped on Benny and morphed him into green leaves.

"Hey!" Benny called out, looking down at his little body.

"Idiot!" Camo said, smacking his own head. "That maneuver's confidential. . . ."

"No, it's secret. This one's confidential," Cloak argued, changing Benny into polka-dotted tree bark, then pink and purple candy stripes.

"Sammy, get them off me!" Benny screamed, jumping onto Samson's head.

"Enough!" Camo yelled to Cloak. "No more!"

"Oh? Show 'em the super-top-secret 'no more'?" Cloak asked. "Gotcha!" he said with a smile and—*ping*—turned Benny invisible except for his eyes and teeth.

"No!" Camo moaned.

But Samson lit up like a bulb. "I've got an idea!" the big lion exclaimed.

Chapter 32

Inside the wildebeests' cave, Nigel was basking in the glow of their worship.

"Him! Him! Him!" the wildebeests chanted as they pushed Larry, Bridget, and Ryan from the holding area.

Bridget stopped stumbling and planted her hooves. She stood up straight and said to the herd, "Who is this Great Him, anyway? I'm the Great Her!"

As they were led toward the throne, Bridget's voice grew louder. "I'll show Him a thing or two," she said. "I mean, I'm from New York, for Pete's sake!"

From the corner of her eye, Bridget saw Larry's and Ryan's stunned expressions. She finally took her eyes off the herd and turned to see the Great Him.

"You have got to be kidding me," she said flatly.

Sitting on the throne, wearing a pineapple crown and waving his plastic torch, was Nigel. He hopped down and approached the group.

Bridget leaned down and looked her ex-zoo-mate in the eye.

"Nigel," she said, furious, "I don't know what you're trying to pull, but I will kick your—"

"Silence!" Nigel bellowed, hitting her on the head with his torch.

Bridget gasped. "Why, you little—"

Nigel raised his torch and bonked her again. "Silence! You do not speak to me!"

Ryan was in shock. "Nigel, what's the deal?" the young lion asked as Bridget stepped back.

"Great Him," Kazar said to Nigel, "shall we prepare the feast?"

Nigel brightened, and he raised his torch. "Yes, we shall! Prepare the feast!" he ordered. "What's on the menu?"

"Them," Kazar said, pointing to Larry, Bridget, and Ryan.

"Oh . . . ," Nigel said, pausing for a moment. "So I can be worshipped as a god or my friends can live? God . . . friends . . . god . . . friends . . ."

Suddenly, Nigel's little torch went out. "Oh, that's subtle," he said, looking up.

Kazar bellowed, "Prepare the meat fire!"

Larry, Bridget, and Ryan held their breath as the wildebeests fired up the grilling stone.

"But WAIT!" Nigel called out. He held on to his

pineapple crown and jumped back on his throne, stalling for time. "We cannot cook them without . . . ONIONS!" The herd stared at their koala god.

"Onions! Onions! Onions! Onions!" the wildebeests chanted.

Blag came forward with an onion stuck on his horn.

"Wow," Nigel said to himself as Blag tossed the onion onto a red stone. "That was fast."

"Let the ritual begin!" Kazar said as the drooling wildebeests watched the onion sizzle, then moved toward Bridget, Larry, and Ryan.

Bridget shot Nigel a look. "I am so mad at you!" she whispered.

"Wait!" Nigel shouted again. The herd froze. "We also need hats. Do we not have the party hats of death?" he asked. He patted his pineapple. "I've got mine!"

The wildebeests looked at each other, confused. Nigel knew he was on sketchy ground.

"And before the feast," he added nervously, "we must all—agggh!" Nigel screamed. His throne was suddenly rising in the air and spinning wildly. "Levitate and spin uncontrollably!" he yelled, holding on to his throne. "And feel a little sick."

"Okay. This is freaky," Larry said, nodding at Bridget and Ryan.

The wildebeests could see nothing holding up the throne. "Oh, Great Him, we are humbled by your power!" they said. They stood on their hind legs and began hopping in circles.

A voice called out over the clatter of hooves. "Pssst. Guys!"

"Look, a squirrel," Larry said.

Bridget and Ryan turned. "Benny?" they both said at once.

"Shhh," Benny told them. "We've got a plan! Follow me!"

Benny scurried behind some rocks as the rest of the gang tiptoed after him.

Feeling woozy, Nigel rocked from side to side in the spinning throne. "I spin to show the whirligig of time and space and matter!" the little koala howled just as a fissure in the volcano opened up.

"Volcanic gas!" Cloak the chameleon called out.

The eruption startled the chameleons. "Evasive maneuvers!" screamed Cloak and Camo as the panicked chameleons scattered.

As they fled, the shape of Samson appeared under the throne. For a moment the big lion froze and didn't know what to do.

"Well, it's about time you got here," said a relieved Nigel. He was ready for some help.

The wildebeests stared at Samson. He was holding up Nigel with his huge paw. "Awww . . . Great Him," Kazar said, delighted, "it's another miracle. You've delivered us . . . a real lion!"

As Samson's eyes searched the cave for an escape, he saw Ryan and his friends getting away!

Kazar turned to Blag. "Your luck has turned," he said, suddenly in a generous mood. "Thanks to the Great Him, we shall all ascend tonight."

Samson knew they were going to begin searching for Ryan and the gang. And when they found them, they'd cook them up and call themselves carnivores.

"Nigel," Samson said, "we gotta create a distraction."

Nigel gave the lion a quick salute and yelled, "Stop!" to the giant wildebeests. "Stand back as the Great Me tenderizes the lion, over seventy-three times my size!" Blag and the rest of the herd stared, mesmerized, as Nigel leaped onto Samson's back.

"Whoooo! Whooo! Whooo!" Nigel howled as he whacked his tiny paws against Samson's head.

Ryan heard the noise and turned to see his father. "Dad?" he cried. "Dad!"

"Ryan, SHHH!" Benny said.

But Ryan wouldn't listen. "My dad made it! My dad's alive!" he exclaimed, and rushed toward Samson.

"Ryan, no!" Benny pleaded, but nothing helped. The spunky squirrel shook his head and sighed, "Oh, boy."

At the center of the cave, Nigel was still pounding away on Samson. "Aaaaiiiiaaagh! Whack, whack, whack, whack, whack!" Nigel shouted fiercely.

Samson looked up for a moment to make sure it was working when he heard Ryan yell, "Dad!"

"Ryan!" Samson roared, whipping his head up and tossing Nigel into the air.

The wildebeests watched their sacred koala sail high above them. Nigel landed with a thud, his pineapple crown falling halfway down his head. "I planned that," he said, assuring the crowd.

Samson was in a panic. "Ryan, no!" he shouted as Ryan fearlessly ran to his side. The wildebeests stomped their feet and closed in around Samson and Ryan.

"Come on, Dad," Ryan said boldly, "let's show these jerks who's at the top of the food chain!"

Kazar turned to Ryan and Samson. "Let's eat the brat first," he said, smiling, as his eyes took on a fierce red glow.

"Over my dead body," Samson growled, protecting his son. He reared back with lightning speed and slashed at Kazar. Kazar's head whipped to the side, where it met with another shattering jolt from Samson's other paw. As Kazar's head swung back, one of his huge horns snapped and fell to the ground. Ryan was watching in amazement when it landed at his feet.

In a fury, the crazed wildebeest lunged at Samson, carrying him up the stone steps and pushing him to the edge of a precipice. Samson dug in his claws, barely able to hold on.

Benny looked on, frantic. He turned to his friends. "He's gonna kill Samson if we don't do something!"

Larry stuck his head up. "Why don't we use the secret play?" he said to everyone. He saw how surprised they were and shrugged. "I know, shut up, Larry, that's stupid," he said, rolling his eyes.

"Yes," Benny exclaimed, "but brilliant stupid!"

Samson clung to the edge of the cliff as Kazar smiled. "They laughed at me when I spoke of the Omen. But look who's laughing now," Kazar sneered. The mighty beast stomped on Samson's paws and laughed maniacally, then shouted, "Next floor . . . the bottom of the food chain!"

As Kazar gloated, Larry, Bridget, Benny, and Nigel were busy putting the secret play into action. They'd stretched Larry across two stalagmites, turning him into a slingshot. They loaded up a rock and pulled back hard.

Chapter 35

"**L**ittle to the left," Nigel said, helping Bridget and Benny take aim. "Fire!" he shouted, with a thumbs-up. Ryan's heart was filled with hope.

The rock shot off Larry like a missile. It hit a stalactite high above Kazar, causing the huge rock formation to crack in several places.

Kazar was angrier than ever. As he moved in to ram Samson over the edge, the gang's sailing rock hit him on the nose. In that moment, Samson managed to climb back onto the ledge.

An enraged Kazar flipped Samson onto his back and was about to do away with the lion, but a stalactite fell, throwing off his focus.

Samson ran up the steps of the koala throne. Kazar followed the lion and jumped on him again.

"We gotta find something bigger," Benny said as they watched the two huge animals battle.

"I know where we can find something bigger," said Ryan, walking over to the gang with a determined look on his face. He leaned against Larry and gave the snake a wink.

The little gang pulled back on Larry as hard as they could. With Ryan in place at the center, the slingshot maneuver was ready to save the day again.

On the steps, Kazar flipped Samson onto his back again. "You should have stayed at home. Now our shrine will become your tomb!" Kazar bellowed, ready to ram Samson and finish him off.

The huge wildebeest snorted and lowered his head as Ryan flew through the air. "Dig deep," Ryan said to himself and *ROARRRRRR*ED!

Chapter 36

Kazar froze as Ryan's fearsome roar vibrated through the cave.

"Ryan!" Samson shouted with pride. Ryan landed on Kazar's back, digging in his claws.

The stunned wildebeest bucked, throwing Ryan against a wall. Samson saw Ryan lying unconscious on the floor of the cave.

Kazar shook his head. "It saddens me when a parent outlives his child," he said to Samson with an evil smile, "even if it is just for a few seconds. . . ."

"Get away from my son!" Samson said, attacking Kazar with all his might. He hurled the wildebeest against the huge koala shrine. Kazar tried to stand, but he was too weak.

The rest of the herd closed in around Samson and Ryan.

"Ryan? Are you still with me?" Samson asked.

Ryan opened his eyes and answered weakly, "It's okay, Dad. I just want you to know . . . I'm sorry you didn't have a father . . . like the one I have. . . ."

"How touching," Kazar sneered as he pulled himself up. "But then, last words usually are." The twisted wildebeest turned to the herd. "Finish them!" he ordered.

The herd didn't move. Kazar was astounded. "I command you to attack them," he shouted loudly, "like true predators!"

Blag stepped forward. "We're tired of pretending to be something we're not," he said defiantly. "But most of all, we're tired of you!"

Blag nodded to another wildebeest, who kicked the sacred stuffed koala toward Kazar.

"Blag!" Kazar said in shock as the stuffed animal landed at his feet. He looked at the herd and scowled. "Fine! I'll kill them myself!"

Now Kazar was seething. The old warrior held up his fallen horn like a knife and started moving toward Samson.

Ryan, still weak, called out to his father. "Dad, remember what you always told me in your stories. Dig deep."

Samson had almost forgotten those words.

At that moment, Kazar moved forward like a speeding freight train. He had charged to within an inch of Samson's nose when Samson let out a wondrous roar. The vibrations sent Kazar careening into the huge koala shrine, shattering it into a million pieces.

Benny covered his ears and cheered on his best friend. "Yeah, baby," said the loyal squirrel.

"Wow," said Ryan, looking up at his fierce father with pride.

To Samson's surprise, the roaring didn't stop; it got louder and louder as the mountain trembled. Samson realized that the volcano was beginning to come apart. He needed to lead his son and his friends to safety.

"Let's go!" Samson called out to Ryan and his friends.

Ryan limped down the stone steps with Samson at his side. Benny, Nigel, Bridget, and Larry were up ahead. Even the wildebeest herd was scrambling for the exit.

But before he left, Blag had something he needed to say. The abused dance student turned to Kazar. "And for the record," he scoffed as rubble began to fall, "I've always hated your choreography. It's so eighties."

Kazar raised his head. "That's right!" He nodded. "Run! Run like the cowardly prey that you are! I will hunt you down!"

Kazar could see that the great shrine was about to fall on him.

He heard Samson yell, "Everyone to the boat!" as the animals evacuated.

As the rumbling grew louder, Kazar yelled, "Top of the food chain!" Suddenly, he stumbled and fell.

The last words Kazar ever heard came from the *I Like You* koala toy. "I'm so cuddly. I like you. . . . I'm so cuddly. I like you. . . . ," it sang as the mountain fell down around the tyrant.

From the deck of their boat, Samson and his crew watched the volcano erupt.

"At least I saw the Wild before it disappeared," said Ryan, standing by his father's side.

"I can still see it," said Samson, with an arm around his son. "It's right . . ."

"Here," said Ryan, pointing to his heart. "I found my roar."

Samson pulled his son in close for a big hug. "We both did, son," he said proudly.

He looked over his shoulder. The entire herd of wildebeests was crowded into the back of the same boat that had taken the gang to the Wild.

"You know, Dad," said Ryan with a smile, "this will be our first story of Samson and Ryan the Wild."

"Right." Samson laughed, shaking his head. "I don't think anybody's going to believe it."

The volcano let out a huge belch as the boat chugged away from the island. Suddenly, the volcano spewed out a smoking black object. It was headed right for the boat. "Incoming!" Ryan shouted.

The wildebeests on deck parted, leaving Nigel to stare up at the falling black object alone. Nigel froze in terror, until the missile landed at his feet. His little eyes narrowed as he picked it up.

"I'm so cuddly. . . . I'm so cuddly. . . . ," the object squawked.

All the animals on deck held their breath, sure that Nigel was going to throttle the charred doll.

"Yes, I know you're cuddly," Nigel said calmly. "But can you float?" he asked, pitching the doll overboard.

In midair, the doll sang, *"I'm having a . . ."*

". . . really nice day, really nice day, really nice day," the wildebeests sang along. Soon the rest of the crew joined in.

Nigel gave the wildebeests a smile and formed them into a chorus line.

"Step-kick-left!" Nigel said, leading the dancing wildebeests. "And step-kick-right!"

The boat rocked as Nigel and the wildebeests danced from side to side.

In the wheelhouse, Cloak and Camo nodded in approval at Larry. He was wearing a basket of fruit on his head like Carmen Miranda.

"Stupendous! Operation snake-over is now complete," exclaimed Cloak.

"You make a fine undercover operative, Agent Larry," Camo agreed.

"Guess what, everybody? I'm a secret agent!" an excited Larry called out.

Benny stood on top of the wheelhouse and looked out to sea. Bridget was at his side. Benny turned to her with a swagger and said, "I get it. You're more than just a tall, lanky goddess. You're a strong, independent female. You don't need to be defined by your relationship, and I respect that."

"It's about time," said Bridget, leaning over and giving Benny the great big giraffe kiss he had been waiting for.

Benny was stunned. "Wh-wh-what was that?" he asked her.

Bridget smiled. "Just your daily dose of vitamin Bridget, baby!"

On deck, Nigel had taught Blag to break-dance. The other wildebeests excitedly formed a circle around Blag as he freestyled.

"Go, Blag! Go, Blag! Go, Blag!" the wildebeests chanted.

That did it. Samson had to get out on the floor and dance. He was so happy.

"Hey, Blag, make some room," he said as he took center stage with an old-fashioned soft-shoe.

"Dad!" shouted Ryan from the sidelines, slightly embarrassed by his father's dancing.

Samson stopped dancing long enough to ask the group how he looked. "Pretty crazy, right? Pretty wild?"

Benny was about to disagree and tell his friend how he really looked, but it was too late. Everyone on the boat had started following Samson's moves and was having a great time.

"This is gonna be a long ride home," sighed Benny, smiling as the boat rocked all the way back to New York.